The Very Grumpy Sloth

Written by Nawal Kalra

Illustrated by Jeevna Kaur

Designed by Mehma B

...for all our beloved grumpy ones...

Gertie slumped at home in a state of some kind.

Sighing...

Brooding...

Whining...

The saddest sloth you'd ever find.

"Hey there grumpy Gertie!," her mama came to say.
"Go out and play! Find your smile, it'll brighten your day!"

It dawned on Gertie, "yes Mama's right!
My smile it's gone! Nowhere in sight!"

"I've lost it, I must have, where can it be?
I have to go look, I have to go see!"

So off she went,
determined as ever
to find the smile,
it was **now or never.**

"Hey Gertie," said Fred, "come on, let's play!"

She grumbled and mumbled and stomped away.

"I'm looking for something, don't stand in my way!"

She looked under the rocks and behind the bush.

She saw mud, some bugs, and a whole lot of mush.

"Hey Gertie," said Milo,
"come on, let's chat!"
She grumbled and
mumbled and said out flat,
"I can't, I can't, I have no
time for that!"

She looked in the hole that ran deep in the ground. "It's lost, it's lost! Nowhere to be found!"

"Hey Gertie," said Sunny, "come on, let's sit!"

She grumbled and mumbled and cried in a fit.

"I can't, I can't, not till I find it!"

She looked under the log and by the stream.
Her smile was nowhere, or so it seemed.

Confused, but amused, her friends followed behind, wondering what in the world Gertie was trying to find.

They watched her search, and they understood, poor Gertie was miserable! She didn't look good.

Perhaps all she needed was a few helping hands.

So they huddled together, hatching plans.

"I GIVE UP!"

Gertie said as she sat
with a plop.
"It's gone, I'm sure.
I really must stop!"

There Gertie sat, staring at her reflection, until she heard noises that perked her attention.

From the water she
saw, three faces come up
behind, with *wagging tongues,*
googlie eyes, and *funny sounds*
of many a kind. Gertie couldn't help
it, she started to giggle. At first
just a bit, then they started to
wiggle!

She laughed and laughed, clear and loud, grinning from ear to ear!

She caught her reflection and saw her smile saying, "I found it, it's here!"

"My smile was lost, but now it's back!
I have you, my friends, to thank for that."

"Oh Gertie, you silly," they claimed with big grins,
"smiles are easy to find, if you just look within!"

Printed in Great Britain
by Amazon